Radio Man

Alan Langer

Table of Contents

Dedication

To all those who had similar experiences and those who were not fortunate enough to return home. To all my brothers and sisters who gave a part of their lives for their country. We have a bond that will forever hold us together because of what we were and what we became.

May we never forget those who didn't make it home.

Acknowledgment

I want to express my deepest gratitude to the following individuals whose support and encouragement have been invaluable throughout the writing of this book.

To my good friend, Joe MacNeil, whose unwavering belief in me and encouragement kept me motivated to continue writing, thank you for your constant inspiration. To my wife, Rose, whose patience and understanding in dealing with my occasional lapses of focus have been a source of strength, your support has meant the world to me.

I also want to thank my grandchildren, whose presence in my life brings me immeasurable joy and strength to carry on.

A special thank you to my dialysis team, whose care and interest in me made the three days a week of dialysis bearable.

Finally, I acknowledge the power that has given me the strength to accept and understand the experiences I've gone through and the wisdom to share them with others.

Prologue

Every soldier who finished a tour of duty in Vietnam has a different view of that experience in their life. The sights and sounds of their experience affected everyone in ways that sometimes cannot be told. I have talked to others who were in Vietnam who didn't like discussing details of their experience. Those who talked freely about their experience spent little time in the field. They spent their time in a base camp.

We were all very young and saw and did things that the people back in "the world" would not be able to understand. We came home to find our country opposed to everything we had fought for. We just wanted to be normal again, to fit in. Some of us managed, and others were not able to adjust. As hard as we try, we will never forget what took place over there. The details took place so very long ago. Names and locations are lost in our memories.

Vietnam was close to the size of California. There were mountains, marshes, grassy areas, oceans, and Islands. The weather was hot and dry for part of the year, rainy and wet the rest of the time. One thing I can say is that I never saw snow.

The guy on the left and the right would give his life for you, and we would have done the same for him. This is probably why Vietnam vets have such strong feelings about their experience.

This is the story of how I remembered that time in my life. Some things were left out due to the painful memories it brought out, but the stories I wanted to tell are here.

Chapter 1
The Early Years

I was born in Montreal, Canada. It was a city that knew cold winters and hard work. My parents were the kind of people who never complained, even when life was tough. They worked long hours at a factory in the garment industry. They didn't make much money, but ensured my brother and I had what we needed. Our house wasn't fancy, and we didn't have many luxuries, but we never went without. My parents always put family first. They worked day after day, to provide a good life for us.

When I was young, they decided we needed a change. Montreal, with its long, cold winters and constant struggle, wasn't the place they saw for us. They dreamed of something better, something warmer. So, we packed up and moved to Los Angeles, hoping for a fresh start. The decision wasn't easy, but it felt like the right one.

My Parents

Los Angeles was a whole new world. The weather was perfect almost every day. The sun was always out, and the warmth felt welcome after Montreal's freezing winters. It wasn't just the weather that made LA special; it was everything. The beaches were beautiful, and there was something magical about the sound of the ocean. The city was alive with the music of the 60s, and it felt like anything was possible. The streets were full of people who were just as laid-back and carefree as the weather. It was a place where you could be whoever you wanted to be.

Life in LA felt easy. My brother and I quickly made friends. We spent our days outside, riding bikes, playing on the beach, and exploring. We didn't worry about much. School was just a part of the day, but it wasn't the focus. It was a time when life seemed full of endless possibilities. Everyone was caught up in the fun of the 60s—the music, the freedom, the excitement of being young. It was a good time to be alive, and I felt lucky to be there.

But even in a place like Los Angeles, a shadow was hanging over everything. As I got older, I started to feel it. The Vietnam War was everywhere. On TV, in the newspapers, and in the conversations I overheard. It was hard to avoid the fact that there was a war going on. And it was hard to ignore the pressure that came with being a young man at that time. The government could draft you into the army if you weren't in school. You could be sent to Vietnam whether you were ready for it or not. It was a real fear for a lot of guys, and it made everything feel a little more serious.

I didn't enjoy school. I wasn't bad at it, but I just didn't care. I didn't want to sit in a classroom every day. The idea of being stuck in school while the world was changing around me didn't sit right. I wanted to be out there, experiencing life. I wanted to travel, see new places, and do something exciting. The idea of going to Vietnam didn't scare me as much as it probably should have. Honestly, the idea of joining the army and getting away from the daily grind of life felt like an adventure. It felt like a way out.

The pressure was always there. You could feel it, even if no one talked about it directly. Young men were expected to go to school; if they didn't, they'd get drafted. It didn't matter if you wanted to or not. You had no choice. I wasn't excited about the war, but I couldn't ignore it. I didn't want to just sit back and wait to be drafted. I didn't want to be like everyone else, just waiting for life to happen. I wanted to be the one who made the choice, who took control of my own path.

Living in LA was great, but deep down, I felt like I needed something more. I wanted to break free from the ordinary, from what everyone else was doing. I wanted to do something that mattered, something bigger than what I could see in my everyday life. Even with the danger and fear it carried, the idea of the army felt like an opportunity. It was a chance to leave everything behind and step into something new.

At that time, it felt like the world was pushing me toward a decision. I couldn't stay in the comfort of LA forever. There was something bigger calling me, something that would change my life forever. And soon enough, I would have to make that choice. The draft was real, and it was coming for young men like me. But I wasn't just going to let it happen to me. I was going to make my way. The adventure was waiting, and I was ready to take the first step toward it.

Chapter 2
The Decision

It all started on an ordinary day when I walked past the recruiting office. I wasn't planning to stop, but something made me walk in. I can't really explain it. Maybe it was the uncertainty, the feeling that I was at a crossroads, or the thought that this could be the change I was looking for. Whatever it was, I found myself stepping into that small, gray building with a sign that said "U.S. Army Recruiting."

The sergeant on duty that day was surprisingly nice. He didn't seem like someone you'd expect to find at a recruiting office. He was friendly and patient and didn't try to push me into anything. He just handed me brochures filled with all kinds of information about the army. He explained that I'd have to go through eight weeks of basic training if I decided to join. After that, I could choose a training school for a specialized skill, which would set me up for a future in the electronics position.

Poster on Recruiting Office

I was interested in the radio repair school he told me about. I didn't know much about it, but the idea of working with radios, and learning something technical and hands-on appealed to me. I took the brochures and left the office, my mind buzzing with thoughts. I wasn't sure if this was the right move, but it was the kind of chance that didn't come often. So I went home, still thinking about it, weighing my options. I didn't talk to anyone about it that night. I just lay there, turning over the idea in my head.

The next day, I went back. I don't know why, but something told me to go in again. So, I did. I walked back into the recruiting office and, without much hesitation, I signed my name. Just like that, I was swearing in, committing to the U.S. Army. It felt like an odd mix of excitement and fear. I wasn't sure what I was getting myself into, but I knew I couldn't turn back now. The call was made.

I went home, full of energy, ready to tell my parents. But the excitement quickly turned into a knot in my stomach when I thought about how they would react. My mother was the first to hear. When I told her, she was shocked, upset even. She couldn't understand why I'd make such a decision. "You're going back to Canada," she said, her voice thick with emotion. "You're not doing this."

I tried to explain, but there was no convincing her. She didn't want me to leave, didn't want me to face whatever lay ahead in the army. But in my heart, I knew I wasn't going back to Canada. I had made my choice, and my home was here now—on this path, in this country. I wasn't about to turn around and go back to the life I'd left behind.

In two weeks, I would go to Fort Ord for basic training. My father didn't say much. He just drove me downtown to the swearing-in ceremony, like it was something he had to do, not something he wanted to do. We didn't talk much in the car. When we arrived, he gave me a simple "Good luck" and left. There was no fanfare, no deep conversation, just a brief hug and a few quiet words before he drove off.

I sat there with thirty other guys, all of us waiting for the bus to take us to Fort Ord. We stayed there all day, not talking much, just waiting. Everyone had their own thoughts, their own feelings about what was happening. We were all in the same boat now, but no one really knew what the water would be like once we set sail.

I must have dozed off while waiting. I don't know how long I'd been asleep, but I felt a presence next to me. I opened my eyes and saw my brother standing there. He had come to see me off. He didn't say much either, but he hugged me tightly. I could feel the weight of the moment in that hug—the love, the uncertainty, the goodbye. It was a simple gesture, but at that moment, it meant everything. "Goodbye," he said softly before turning to leave. I watched him walk away, feeling the sting of the goodbye in my chest.

I was about to leave for a world that was so far from anything I had ever known. All the excitement and fear I felt in that moment were a mix of the unknown—what was waiting for me at Fort Ord, what would happen in the coming weeks, and what the future would hold. It was a crossroads, and I was standing right in the middle, ready to take the first step into a journey that would change everything.

My Brother

Chapter 3
Trip to Fort Ord

The bus ride to Fort Ord felt like it lasted forever. We sat there, packed together, each of us lost in our thoughts, none speaking much. The air was thick with uncertainty. No one knew what to expect, and that was perhaps the hardest part. Basic training wasn't something any of us could truly understand until we lived through it. We'd heard the stories—the rumors, the nightmares about sadistic drill sergeants who would break you down just to build you back up. Some of the guys whispered nervously, imagining the worst. Would the sergeants be as tough as they'd heard? Would I even be able to make it through? I was in decent shape, but this was something else entirely. I'd never been through the kind of grueling, intense training that was waiting for us. The thought made my stomach twist in knots.

We were all silent, but a thousand questions circled in our minds. Was I really cut out for this? What if I couldn't handle it? But no one said anything. We just stared out the windows at the passing night, the city lights dimming behind us as we left everything we knew behind.

Finally, after hours, the bus pulled into Fort Ord. It was late, the night air was crisp, and the base looked quiet outside. We stopped in front of a small, nondescript building. Everyone shuffled their feet, waiting in a tense silence, unsure of what was next. We had no idea what we were in for, but we knew this was the point of no return. The moment we stepped off that bus, everything would change.

And then, the door to the building opened. A drill sergeant appeared in the doorway, his silhouette cutting through the dim light. He took his time walking toward the bus, almost like he was enjoying the tension he'd built up. It wasn't until he climbed aboard that he finally spoke.

"Welcome to Fort Ord, gentlemen," he said, his voice steady, calm, almost warm, like a teacher greeting his students on the first day of class. "You will be with us for the next eight weeks."

We looked at each other, nodding, trying to make sense of the words, still unsure whether we were about to face hell or something slightly less intimidating. But before we could process what he'd said, his smile vanished. It disappeared faster than the California sun setting over the horizon, replaced with a scowl that could stop a man's heart. Without missing a beat, he yelled, his voice echoing through the bus.

"You have 20 seconds to get off this fuckin' bus. MOVE!"

And just like that, the calm before the storm was over. We shot up from our seats, practically tumbling over one another to get out the door. We weren't even sure where we were supposed to go, but we followed the line in front of us, the urgency of his voice forcing our legs to move before our minds even had time to catch up.

The chaos continued as we lined up outside, standing at attention, hearts racing, adrenaline flooding our veins. And then the sergeant made his way down the line. The insults started immediately. It was relentless—each one more creative and cutting than the last. We were like cattle being herded through an invisible gate, just waiting for the next verbal slap across the face. The atmosphere was thick with tension. But none of us could stop looking at the ground, the grass beneath our feet, just waiting for the moment we could breathe again.

When he got to me, I couldn't help it. I didn't mean to, but a grin crept onto my face. Something about the whole scene—the way he moved, the way he spoke—struck me as absurd. I had never heard anyone talk like that before, and it made me smile for some reason. A quick, nervous smile, but a smile nonetheless.

When I smiled, the sergeant's eyes locked onto mine like a predator spotting its prey. "What the fuck are you smiling at?" he snapped, his voice like a whip. I froze, feeling the blood drain from my face. I tried to explain, tried to tell him I wasn't mocking him, but before I could say anything, he punched me in the stomach. Before I even realized what had happened, my body hit the ground hard, the air knocked out of me. I could hear him above me, still yelling insults at the others as he stepped right over me like I wasn't even there. It was like I had become part of the dirt beneath me, nothing more than another obstacle in his way.

When he finally finished with the line, he called out a few names, mine included. "You girls, follow me," he barked. "You're going to the alien barracks."

I blinked, confusion flooding my mind. Alien? I had been called a lot of things in my life—stupid, lazy, maybe even naïve—but "alien"? That was new. What the hell did that even mean? It didn't matter though. I was still trying to recover from the shock of hitting the ground and realizing that this was just the beginning.

We were told we had to go through extra processing because we weren't U.S. citizens—something I hadn't really thought about until then. We had to be cleared before going to "The Hill," as they called it, for our real training. They didn't want to waste any time on us; they just tossed us into the corner while they figured out what to do with us. Alien barracks—whatever that meant—seemed like the place where everyone who wasn't from around here got tossed who didn't quite fit in.

So, we marched—well, shuffled—our way to the barracks. The night was still young, but it felt like the longest night of my life. The first authentic taste of military life had just been served, and there was no going back.

Chapter 4
The Alien Barracks

The first thing they did when we arrived was march us to what they called the "alien barracks." I wasn't sure what to expect, but nothing could have prepared me for the reality of it. It felt like stepping into another world, a place completely foreign to everything I had known so far. We were to stay there until we were cleared, a process that stretched on for what felt like forever—four long days of confusion, frustration, and loneliness.

The barracks were a strange mix of people—an odd assortment of men from all corners of the world. Some could barely speak English, their faces full of fear and uncertainty. Others didn't seem to belong anywhere, men who had been judged unfit for the hill, for the real army life ahead of us. It was a holding place, a temporary shelter for people who didn't quite fit in anywhere else.

Among them were bed-wetters—grown men, some even older than me, struggling with shame they couldn't hide. There were homosexuals struggling with their own demons and secrets in a place where such things were anything but accepted. And then there were the mentally unstable—those whose minds had been broken by whatever burden they had carried with them into this life. The barracks were a bizarre cross-section of humanity, a collection of souls thrown together for reasons we couldn't quite understand.

At night, the place was alive with sounds that kept you awake long after you'd settled into your cot. Some men would pace up and down the hallways, muttering to themselves in a language that only they seemed to understand. Their voices echoed in the dark, and though I tried not to look, I could feel the weight of their insanity pressing against me. It made the walls feel closer; the air feel heavier.

Then there were the cries. Some of the men cried all night long, their sobs a constant reminder that not everyone was ready for the life we were about to live. The fear and uncertainty got to them in a way that I couldn't even begin to understand. I'd lie in my bed, staring at the ceiling, feeling utterly helpless and lonely. I had no one to talk to or who understood what I was going through. All I had was the sound of my thoughts and the feeling of time dragging on with no end.

Each day, we marched. That was all we did. Endless marching—march here, march there, repeat. They told us it was part of the process. They were going to break us down, they said, to strip us of everything we thought we knew. And those of us who would make it to The Hill, to real army life, would be rebuilt in the army's image. It was hard to imagine any of this leading to something better. But it didn't matter. We had no choice. Marching, screaming, pushing through the exhaustion—this was our life now.

The days felt like they would never end. The others, the crybabies, would talk endlessly about how hard it was on The Hill, how brutal it would be. They'd tell us about the drills, the rules, the constant pressure to be perfect. I couldn't relate to their fear. Maybe I didn't fully grasp what was coming, but I couldn't help but feel that they were just making it sound worse than it was.

And then there was the guy who thought he knew all the tricks. There's always one. He was a little older than the rest of us, with a way about him that made him seem like he had been around for a while. He told us he could get us out of the army, that he knew all the loopholes, the backdoor deals, the tricks that could get us discharged before we even saw the front lines. For just $25, he promised he could get me out. I didn't laugh in his face, but I wanted to. Little did he know, I had already made my choice. I signed up for this. I didn't need an escape. I was here for the ride—no matter where it took me.

At that moment, I knew I was in the right place. With all its strangeness and madness, the alien barracks was just the beginning.

Whatever came next, I was ready for it. I had already decided to take control of my own fate. No tricks, no escapes. Just the army and the man I was about to become.

Chapter 5
Basic Training

The day had finally come. A cattle car came to pick us up, and with it, a sense of nervous anticipation. We were about to leave behind the comfort of the civilian world and enter the rigid, unforgiving environment of military life. As the truck rolled along, I felt a mix of excitement and dread. Soon, we'd go to the hill, where everything would change. We arrived at the barracks, the place where we would live for the next eight weeks. The atmosphere was tense, and the drill sergeants were there waiting for us, standing like statues, their faces hard, their gazes piercing. There was no warmth in their eyes—just impatience and authority. They were not there to make us feel welcome or comfortable.

"Get the fuck off this truck, now!" one of them barked. It wasn't a question—it was an order. "Line up, faggots!" The word hit me like a slap in the face. One moment, I had been called an "alien," an outsider; now, I was being degraded in front of the others. It was a stark reminder that here, you were nothing but another recruit, another body to be molded into something else that conformed.

We quickly lined up as instructed, feeling the weight of their eyes on us, cold and judgmental. The drill sergeants introduced themselves, their voices sharp and commanding. They led us up to the second floor of the barracks. This would be our home for the next eight weeks—our prison, training, and proving ground. The place where we would either break or become something stronger.

The drill sergeant made it clear from the start—this was no place for mistakes. Under no uncertain terms, we were told never to walk down the middle of the bay. Our large, open room was called a "bay," and only the drill sergeants had the privilege of walking down the center. It was their domain, their space. We were told how to make our beds to the standard they demanded, keep our floor locker neat, and organize our wall locker. Every detail mattered, and every second was scrutinized. If something was off, you could feel the anger behind those cold eyes.

"And now, before supper, we're going for a run," our sergeant announced, and just like that, we were off, running. It felt like it went on forever, our legs burning, our lungs screaming for air. Basic training was designed to break you down—to strip you of everything you knew, everything that made you comfortable—and rebuild you into a soldier. They did this through sleep deprivation, physical training, and constant mental and emotional pressure. You were pushed to the limit, with just enough sleep to keep you functional and just enough energy to keep running, marching, and enduring.

In the mess hall, the food was nothing to celebrate. It didn't matter what was served; you ate it. If you were given Lima beans, like I was one night, you ate them—even if it made you sick. There was no room for complaints. You ate what you were given, and if you didn't, you'd face consequences. Our only day off was Sunday, but that wasn't a true rest day. Even then, there was always something to do—always something to prepare for the next challenge.

Range week was one of the hardest parts of training. It was a brutal test of endurance and willpower. We had to run five miles from our barracks, through sand that seemed to swallow every step we took. There was no quitting, no slowing down. If someone fell behind, you carried them. No one was left behind. A strange kind of solidarity formed during those grueling days, a bond forged in sweat and exhaustion. When that week was finally over, there was a collective sigh of relief, but we knew more to come.

As the weeks passed, the routine became relentless. One final test awaited us: crawling 100 yards through mud while live fire rang overhead. The noise was deafening, the chaos palpable. It felt like the whole world was coming apart above us, but we had to focus, to move forward, no matter what. This was what real combat training was like, I realized. This was what it felt like to be prepared for the worst. The noise, the pressure, the chaos all added up to something bigger than ourselves, something that would stay with us long after we left the training grounds.

I didn't know it yet, but my future would soon take me to places I never expected. Names like Fort Ord and Fort Sill sounded so strange to me now, almost like places in a faraway world. In my mind, I imagined that after radio repair school, I might finally be able to see far-off lands like Germany or Japan—exotic, exciting, and adventure. But Vietnam? It wasn't even on my radar. I had no idea how wrong I was about where I headed next.

Sergeant Martin, our drill sergeant, was a cruel man. He had no patience for us and showed no mercy. His language was harsh, his tone even harsher. Every night, when it was his turn to be in the office, he would come upstairs to ask if we wanted a burger. He'd be heading into town, and we'd hand over our money, trusting that he would return. But he never did. He took our money and disappeared, and we never dared discuss it. Fear and silence ruled the barracks.

Another time, Sergeant Martin decided to have fun with us. Late at night, he blew his whistle. It was a signal for us to rush downstairs and line up. We did as instructed, but he wasn't satisfied. "Too slow," he yelled. "We're doing it again!" We filed back upstairs, our bodies aching from the day's training, only to wait by the door, anticipating the next whistle. We rushed down again when it blew, only to hear his anger rise again. "Too slow!" he barked. "Back upstairs. We're doing it again!" The threat was clear this time: "If you're too slow, you'll come down with your foot locker." Exhausted and frustrated, we climbed back up, waiting for the next round. But the whistle never blew again. We stood by the door, waiting silently, only to realize we had been played. It was a lesson in patience, in endurance, and in the realization that sometimes, in the military, the mind games are just as tough as the physical challenges.

Graduation day finally came. We had survived the madness, the pain, the frustration, and the constant pressure. It was time to get our orders and head home for two weeks before moving on to the next training phase. I knew where I was going next—radio repair school. But I didn't realize that it would be at Fort Sill, Oklahoma. The idea of traveling to a new place, far from home, was both exciting and terrifying.

I couldn't help but think about how far I had come. Fort Ord, Fort Sill—these places were becoming real to me now. They weren't just names on a map but part of my journey. Who knew where this road would take me next? Would I get the chance to travel further? Maybe to Germany or Japan? Or would I end up somewhere I had never expected? The thought of Vietnam never crossed my mind, but I knew it was just around the corner, waiting for me to find out whether I was ready.

The adventure, the uncertainty, and the challenge made me realize that I was no longer the person I had been when I boarded that cattle car. Basic training had changed me in ways I couldn't yet fully understand. But one thing was certain: I was ready for whatever came next.

Chapter 6
Oklahoma

Basic training was finally over. If anything, it had made me stronger, but it hadn't broken me down like they intended. I was still that 18-year-old kid who had enlisted with dreams of excitement and adventure. The past eight weeks felt long, like an eternity away from home, but I had survived it. I had come through tougher than before, but still the same kid deep inside. I still craved the adventure that had pulled me into this life in the first place.

I was about to go home for two weeks before being sent to Fort Sill, Oklahoma, for radio repair school. It felt like a strange kind of freedom, being able to sleep in my own bed again, not having to listen to the constant insults and orders. My mother was always asking where I'd be going after training, but I didn't have any solid answers. I knew I was heading to radio repair school, but beyond that, who could say? If they needed radio repairers in Vietnam, that's where I'd go.

Seeing my friends again was a mix of joy and sadness. We had all changed during my time away, though we didn't quite realize it at first. They were all in college now, doing everything they could to avoid the draft. I had taken another route. So far, I haven't felt like I have made a mistake. But I knew that as we stood there together, laughing and joking as we always did, we had grown apart. It was a quiet realization that life was moving on, and this chapter was closing.

When I arrived at Fort Sill, I was hit with a shock. It was cold, and there was snow on the ground. I wasn't used to the cold, and the march to our classes every morning felt painful. But this wasn't like basic training. The training here was different. We had civilian instructors—no drill sergeants yelling at us, no insults. These instructors were patient and thorough, and treated us with a level of respect I hadn't been used to. They knew we were there to learn, and they made sure we did.

The training lasted six weeks, and when it was over, we gathered outside to hear our orders. It was freezing, but there was an energy in the air. We all stood there, waiting for our names to be called. One by one, they announced where we would be going—some to Germany, some to Japan, some staying stateside. Then, they called my name: "Alan Langer, Vietnam."

There was a mix of emotions inside me. I had always wanted excitement, an adventure to remember, but Vietnam? A war zone? That wasn't exactly the kind of adventure I had imagined. I tried to push the fear down, trying to convince myself that this was just part of the journey, but I couldn't help the anxiety creeping up. I was going to Vietnam.

Before being shipped out, I had 30 days of leave. It was a strange time—like a brief pause before the storm. My parents picked me up from the airport, but the car ride was silent, filled with a kind of tension I couldn't cut through. Finally, my mother broke the silence. "So, where are you going?" she asked. I had to say it out loud. "Vietnam." The tears flowed down her face immediately.

When we got home, she went straight to her room, shut the door, and stayed there for the rest of the night. I could hear her crying from the other side of the door. My brother, who had never really talked to me about anything serious, took me out to dinner that night. It was the first time I had felt so close to him. He asked me all kinds of questions, like if I was scared or if I really wanted to go. I could tell he was just as worried as my mother, but he didn't know how to say it.

Over dinner, he repeated what my mother had said: "You don't have to go." But I knew I couldn't stay. "If I leave and go to Canada, I'll never be able to come back," I told him. That was the reality. We both sat there in silence for a while. The conversation felt more real, more honest than any we'd ever had before. And I guess, in his way, he really did care for me.

That night was a memory I would never forget. The next morning, my mother was in a better mood. We had a real conversation. I told her I was a radio repairman and that I would be stationed at a base camp, away from the front lines. I wasn't going to be in the thick of the fighting. I could see her relax a little bit after that. It wasn't much, but it helped. I think it was important for her to know that I wasn't going to be in immediate danger.

We spent the next couple of days together, but I couldn't shake the feeling that I was leaving something behind. I wouldn't see my friends for a year. That was going to be the most challenging part— being away from home for so long. But we made the most of the time we had. We went out for one last dinner together. I told my parents that my best friend would be taking me out and that he'd drive me to the airport the next morning. It was easier that way, I guess.

We went to the beach after dinner, just like we used to do when we were younger. We watched the sun go down in silence. Neither of us spoke for a long time. Finally, I asked, "What if I don't come home?" He didn't answer right away. It wasn't a question that could be easily answered. We just sat there, staring at the horizon. Finally, he said, "Before your tour in Nam is over, you'll get a picture and a letter from Cam Nelson."

Cam Nelson was a dancer on a popular TV show at the time. My friend had gone to the studio and told them my story. He'd given them my address. And sure enough, a few months later, I received that letter and picture from Cam Nelson.

The next morning, he drove me to the airport. We stopped in front of the entrance, embraced each other without saying much, and that was it. He went off, and I walked through the doors, leaving behind everything I had ever known.

Fort Sill had been cold and unfamiliar, but now I was leaving for something even bigger. Vietnam. I had no idea what to expect, but I knew this would be the most challenging journey I would ever take. As I walked into the airport, I couldn't help but wonder if I would ever come back. But I was ready. This was my path now. And I would follow it wherever it led.

Chapter 7
Processing In

From Los Angeles, I flew up to Washington State. At Fort Lewis, I would process in for my journey to Vietnam. This was it—the next step in a trip I had only dreamed of, but now it was real. We were housed in a large building that resembled a warehouse. Rows of beds stretched out across the space, each one belonging to a soldier who would soon be going overseas. It was cramped and sterile, but it didn't matter. We were all in the same boat, waiting for our orders.

The place felt like a temporary holding cell, and it wasn't long before we started getting used to the rhythm of life there. There were plenty of vending machines for our sweet tooths and several payphones scattered around the room, though we could never really use them the way we wanted. Our calls were always monitored, and we weren't allowed to talk about anything related to where we were, where we were going, or how many of us there were. We could talk about anything else, but those topics were off-limits. Secrecy was of utmost importance.

Three times a day, we were marched by armed guards to the mess hall for our meals and then marched back to the warehouse. It was like a weird, constant cycle—eat, sleep, and wait. But no matter how much we wanted to chat or make small talk, we had to keep everything to ourselves. Even our conversations were guarded. It wasn't paranoia; it was protocol. Everything was under wraps.

Every morning, we'd gather with the rest of the guys to hear the names of those shipping out that day. I was there for five days, just waiting for my name to be called. I had to keep my nerves in check. And when it finally happened, it hit me like a punch to the gut. I had an hour to get ready. In a blink, my adventure was about to begin.

We were driven to the airport in a military vehicle. The mood in the air was different than it had been back at Fort Lewis. There was an electric sense of anticipation, a quiet buzz of what was to come. When we arrived, we boarded a commercial flight, the crew all civilians. They were unbelievably kind to us, like they knew this would be a long and challenging journey for all of us. I could see it in their faces—they were trying to comfort us, to give us something familiar before we faced the unknown. We were just young Americans, a mix of guys who had signed up for the adventure and a few like me who hadn't really thought much about what the war would mean.

I felt like the crew knew what we didn't yet fully understand: this was a one-way trip for some of us. The reality of that hung in the air. Some of the young men on that flight would never return. There was an unspoken sadness in the way the flight attendants looked at us, in the way they moved through the cabin, offering us drinks and snacks as if nothing was different, but they knew.

The trip over was relaxed at first. People talked, joked around, and found camaraderie in the shared experience. We were all in this together now. But as we began to descend into Vietnam, everything changed. The mood in the cabin shifted from lightheartedness to something more serious. There was an unspoken understanding that the fun and games were over. The lights went out as we began to descend in the night, and the reason for that became clear soon enough—so we wouldn't be detected. It was a precaution, but it also served to heighten the tension.

I looked out the window as we got closer to the ground. In the distance, I saw flares descending slowly in the dark sky. They lit up the night like little stars falling from the heavens, casting an eerie glow over the landscape. I turned to the guy sitting next to me, ready to make some offhand comment, but as I glanced at his face, I saw something that made my throat tighten. Tears were running down his cheeks.

That's when it hit me—some guys were taking this seriously. Some guys were scared. They were facing the reality of where we were headed. But for me, this was just the beginning. This was the adventure I had asked for, the excitement I had always dreamed about.

My friends at home? They had no idea what they were missing. This was real. This was happening.

When the plane finally touched down, the crew gave each of us the same parting words: "Good luck, see you in a year." It was a bittersweet farewell. Looking into the stewardess's eyes as she said goodbye to me, I saw something I hadn't expected—sadness. She didn't say much, but I could tell that she had shaken many hands of young men just like me, and some of them wouldn't be coming back. I smiled at her, trying to mask the uncertainty I felt inside. But deep down, I knew what we were all facing.

I walked into the humid, thick Vietnamese night, stepping off that plane and into a world so different from everything I had ever known. My adventure had begun. The lights of the plane faded into the distance behind me and ahead lay only the unknown. Whatever would come next, I was ready for it. Or so I told myself.

Chapter 8
The Nam

The moment I stepped off the plane, I felt it—the intense, suffocating humidity that hit me like a punch to the chest. The air was so thick it felt like I was trying to breathe underwater. Every step I took toward the terminal had me sweating through my clothes. The heat wrapped around me, pressing down with an almost physical weight. I'd never experienced anything like this before—back home in California, the heat was dry, but here, it felt like the air itself was alive and relentless. Sweat poured down my face, and my shirt clung to my back. It was like I was walking through a steam room, but there was no escape.

After the exhausting walk, we were taken to a nearby base where we would stay for the next week. It was already late by the time we arrived, so they told us to get some sleep and rest up for the next day. But sleep was almost impossible in that heat. The humidity wrapped around my body like a blanket, and I couldn't stop sweating, even as I lay there trying to shut my eyes. Every time I moved, I could feel the dampness sticking to me. It was so hot that it felt like the air had weight. I had never experienced anything like it, and it made everything harder. Every time I closed my eyes, I was greeted with nothing but the oppressive warmth. I tossed and turned, restless and frustrated, but eventually, I drifted into a fitful sleep, my body struggling to adapt.

Arriving in Vietnam

In the morning, we were gathered and told about the basics of our time here. We were briefed on what to expect and the dos and don'ts. One of the things they really hammered in was to avoid getting involved with the local women. They warned us that it could lead to serious trouble. Apparently, it wasn't just about personal complications; there were countless background checks and a mountain of forms we'd have to fill out. I didn't quite understand it all at the time, but the seriousness in their tone made it clear that this wasn't something to take lightly.

They also began our training right away. The first thing they wanted us to experience was the patrols. We went out on patrol to learn the basic procedures, how to move in the jungle, and what to do if we encountered enemy forces. The first patrol was an overnight experience, and it was nothing like I had imagined. The terrain was rough and hilly. The jungle was dense, the brush thick and tangled. Every step felt like we were fighting nature itself. We took turns with machetes, hacking our way through the thick underbrush. The air was damp, and the ground was uneven. It was exhausting work, and it made me realize how much more I needed to learn to survive out there.

By late afternoon, we reached our objective, a hill—though I don't remember its name. We were told to dig in, but not at the top of the hill, instead on the side of it. The mission was simple: hold the hill. There were no heavy combat situations, at least not yet. We were all green, inexperienced soldiers, so I figured they weren't going to send us into a dangerous hot zone just yet. It was a test, a way to get us accustomed to the realities of being out in the field.

We dug our foxholes and took turns on guard duty. Two hours on, two hours off to sleep. But sleep didn't come easy. The night felt endless. The jungle around us seemed alive with sounds, the distant rustling of animals and the occasional crack of a branch underfoot. It was unnerving. As I sat in my foxhole, scanning the dark, I felt a deep loneliness that seemed to settle into my bones. The silence was heavy, broken only by the occasional flare lighting up the sky and the distant thud of artillery fire. It felt like there was a firebase somewhere close by. The light from the flares would illuminate the night sky, casting strange, eerie shadows across the jungle, but nothing happened that night. Still, the tension was palpable. It felt like we were being tested, slowly introduced to the reality of what we would face here.

Each day, a few of the guys would be called to leave for their permanent units. I couldn't wait for the day my name would be called. This was the moment I'd been waiting for—the start of my military career. I had my sights set on the communications shack, working with radios, fixing equipment, and being part of something important. I was counting the days. Only 357 days left until I'd return to the

World. Every day, I could feel the weight of that number on my mind. It was a reminder of the time I still had to endure, but also the promise of getting back home one day.

Finally, the call came. My name was on the list. I was going to the Central Highlands, assigned to the 173rd Airborne Brigade. The excitement surged through me. This was it—the next step. I was ready for it. A new chapter had begun, and as I packed up my gear, I couldn't help but feel a sense of nervous anticipation. The journey was only just starting, and I had no idea what was ahead of me, but I was about to find out.

I arrived at LZ English, and my first thought was how massive it was. It was unlike anything I had seen before. The base was oval-shaped, and it stretched on for what felt like miles. On one end, there was a large airfield, a hive of activity with helicopters coming and going. On the other end, there was a chopper pad, the sound of blades cutting through the air almost constant. The whole base probably covered about three kilometers around. It felt so vast and open—yet there was a sense of confinement in the air.

The first thing that really stood out to me was the burn zone that surrounded the base. There was a hundred-yard perimeter of charred land, the brush cleared and burned off. It was an unnatural, sterile look to the land. It felt like the place had been scrubbed clean as if nature had been forced back into some strange battle. Just outside the burn zone, there was a small village next to the airfield. I could see the people going about their daily lives, their homes nestled between the land and the military operation.

I walked into the command post to sign in. The first sergeant was at the desk, and I handed him my papers. He glanced at them, then looked back up at me. "Radio man," he said, barely glancing at the papers.

"No, uh, radio repair man," I corrected him, feeling a little uneasy.

He stared at me for a long moment before repeating in the same sharp tone, "Radio man."

I wasn't sure if it was a mistake or if he was just testing me, but I didn't argue. "Radio repair man," I said again, more firmly.

He didn't say a word for a second, just looked at me like I was wasting his time. Then, without any change in his expression, he bellowed, "I said radio man." The sound of his voice was enough to make anyone jump. "Welcome to The Nam, welcome to the army."

I had no choice now. It was settled. I was going to be carrying a radio out in the field whenever my platoon went out on patrol. It wasn't what I had expected, but there was no backing out now.

There were three types of patrols we did out here: search and destroy, reconnaissance, and ambush. None of them were exactly pleasant, but you couldn't show weakness, not here. Ambush was the worst—usually meant staying out all night, waiting, and hoping you wouldn't get caught. But my first patrol was reconnaissance. The mission was simple enough: we were supposed to look for any signs that the Viet Cong were setting up mortars to fire into the camp.

Map of Vietnam

The whole day was spent walking through thick, oppressive humidity. It felt like the air was thick enough to cut with a knife. It was a relief to get back to camp and take a cold shower. But even as I scrubbed the dirt off my skin, I couldn't shake the feeling that something was always just a step ahead of me—something I couldn't quite see, something I couldn't quite name. The loneliness was a constant companion. I found myself thinking about The World, about home, about everything that wasn't here. The nights were long, and the days dragged on. But, I found that the only real release from the constant boredom and loneliness was to smoke marijuana. It helped me forget, at least for a while. It made the days bearable and easier to handle.

There was one rule, though: never smoke when you're on patrol. You couldn't afford to be slow or distracted when out there in the field.

Our next mission was a search-and-destroy mission. Intelligence had told us that we were likely to make contact in this area, and I have to admit, I was excited. Not scared. Not worried. Just excited. This was it—the real thing. I thought I was ready.

We were walking through some tall brush when the shit hit the fan. The sudden crack of gunshots shattered the air, and before I knew it, all hell had broken loose. I remembered what they had taught us: "If you hear shots, hit the ground." I didn't hesitate. I hit the ground like my life depended on it—because it did.

It was total chaos. Yelling. Bullets flying in all directions. I had no idea where they were coming from. It felt like the world was exploding around me. My heart was pounding in my chest. It was my first real firefight, and it was nothing like I had imagined. The first time I heard a bullet whiz by my head, I thought it was a bee. But it wasn't a bee—it was a bullet. And it sounded just like a pissed-off bee with a vendetta.

It was unnerving, to say the least. The sound was so close I could feel the wind from it. Then, just as suddenly as it started, it went quiet. I lay there, trying to control my breathing, my body frozen, waiting for the next shot to come. I looked over at the guy next to me. He was lying still, his neck covered in blood. He wasn't moving. His eyes were open, staring at nothing.

For a moment, everything froze. My heart stopped for a second, and the reality of the situation hit me. What if that was me? How would my parents feel if they found out? How would anyone? It was a sobering thought. Life, my life, seemed fragile now. The sounds of the jungle, the distant gunfire, the flicker of the flares—it all felt like a bad dream, one that I couldn't wake up from.

Things changed that day. The innocence I had before, the excitement of being here, was gone. I wasn't the same. Something inside of me shifted at that moment, and I realized that I was deep in The Nam now—truly in it, not just playing soldier.

I had no illusions left. Welcome to The Nam.

Choppers became our guardian angels. They were the ones who picked us up, dropped us off, and provided cover when we needed it. The distinctive sound of their blades, that deep, powerful rhythm, was something that never left you. I can still hear it today in the back of my mind. It was the sound of safety—when you heard a chopper, you knew help was on the way. When we had a mission far from camp, a chopper would pick us up and take us there. And when the mission was over, it would come back for us.

Our Guardian Angels

Once, I was asked to go to a fire base to pick up a radio. The chopper took me to a hill that had been leveled at the top. A fire base had been built on that flat spot, a camp that fired artillery. It dropped me off and told the pilot I'd only be a minute. As I made my way to the communications shack, I could hear the blades of the chopper lifting into the air, the sound growing distant. I asked one of the guys there when the chopper would be back.

"In two days," he told me. So, I had to stay there for a while.

It wasn't all bad, though. They gave me earmuffs to wear because the pounding of the guns was overwhelming. Even with the earmuffs on, the sound of the artillery fire was deafening. The pressure from each shot reverberated through the ground and up into my bones. Two days there seemed to stretch on forever. But finally, the chopper returned for me, and on the way back, the pilot asked if I wanted to take a ride.

We flew along the coast, and the beaches below were beautiful. Then, he said, "I'll give you a better view." With that, he dipped the chopper down, flying low just above the water. I started to get nervous, thinking we might actually touch the water. The Viet Cong didn't like the choppers—they were a big problem for them, inflicting severe damage. Because of this, they'd sometimes drop mortars every once in a while, and every so often, they'd get lucky and hit one of the choppers.

During the cold months, the temperature would drop to as low as 70 degrees. It didn't seem cold, but after months of 96 to 105-degree heat, that sudden drop felt like it was freezing. Sitting guard duty in that cold weather was bitter. I would sit in a bunker all night, feeling the chill seep through my clothes. One night, I had smoked quite a bit of marijuana, and I was pretty out of it. I sat bundled up, just staring into the burn zone, watching the wire.

Then I saw something move. I didn't even think about it at first. I just focused on the movement, not realizing it was someone crawling through the wire. It didn't hit me until later that it was a sapper—a trained demolition expert who specialized in crawling through the wire. His mission was to blow something up.

I kept watching him, still too out of it to process what was happening fully. That's when all hell broke loose. The bunkers on either side of me opened fire on the sapper. There wasn't much left after that.

As the end of my tour approached, morale in my unit and all over the base was at an all-time low. People were getting fed up. Some had had enough of the army and the way the war was being fought. Others had gotten caught up in the anti-war movement, hearing all the negative press back home. The worst, though, was being called "baby killers." That label was like a heavy weight that hung around our necks. It took a toll on all of us. Some guys even reenlisted just to escape the attitude at home. The feeling in The Nam was more familiar to them than the cold reception back in the States.

Going back to the world wasn't what we thought it would be. The talk among the guys mostly centered around how many days we had left. When you had 30 days or less, you didn't go out on patrols. Everyone was just counting the days. I thought to myself, No matter how bad it is back home, it can't be worse than being here.

My great big adventure was almost over. It felt like it had lasted a lifetime, but it was coming to an end. I'd probably survive the last 30 days, but I was no longer the same person who had first stepped foot into The Nam. The innocence was gone.

Radio that I carried

Chapter 9
The Pillow

In the camp, there were two main groups, two separate worlds that barely collided—though now and then, tensions would rise. On one side, you had the drinkers. These were the guys who drank beer, listened to country and Western music, and did their best to forget about the war. On the other side were the potheads, who smoked marijuana and listened to the pop music of the day. Each group had its own rhythm, its own set of habits and coping mechanisms. It was easy to pick out who belonged to which group based on what you could hear echoing through the barracks. The two sides didn't get along all the time, but for the most part, they stayed apart. Everyone had their own way of surviving in the madness, and there was little point in getting involved in someone else's escape.

The Vietnamese were incredibly clever when it came to selling us pot. They figured out how to sneak it through the checkpoints and into our hands, sometimes in the most unexpected forms. I saw them stuff marijuana into cigarette packs or cleverly conceal it in small pillows. I remember one time buying a pillow with a pound of pot hidden inside. It cost me $20, and I figured it would be a good way to send some home to my friends. But I kept putting it off, never quite getting around to sending it.

Then, one day, Peter Connor, a guy I'd known around the camp, asked me if he could buy it from me. I agreed and sold it to him for the same $20 I paid. In my mind, it was a small loss; I figured I could always get another one if I wanted it. But it wasn't long before things went sideways. Just before Peter was about to send the pillow home, there was a raid. The base authorities didn't mind us smoking pot, but every now and then, they had to show they were doing something about the drug problem. They needed to look good for the higher-ups, so they'd stage these raids. And, of course, Peter got caught.

He was arrested and thrown into the base jail while waiting for his hearing. When the day came, there was no defense—he was caught red-handed. He was sentenced to six months in LBJ—Long Binh Jail, just outside Saigon. The place was notorious for its cruelty, run by Marines who had a serious disdain for Army personnel. Six months there could feel like an eternity.

The company commander called me in. He told me that I'd be escorting Peter to Long Binh. There would be two of us taking him. The captain was clear about the rules: "If he runs, shoot him." I nodded, not saying a word. I agreed to the terms, though deep down, I couldn't imagine shooting him for trying to escape. Where could he go? I thought. There was no way out of the country, not unless he had a plane hidden somewhere.

We boarded a plane headed south. As soon as we were airborne, I took off Peter's handcuffs. It wasn't necessary, not really. But we were both aware of the situation we were in. We had planned to stay at Cam Ranh Bay Air Base for a couple of days. Peter was quiet the entire trip, subdued in a way that made sense. I don't blame him— Long Binh Jail wasn't somewhere anyone would want to go.

The entire time we were flying down, I felt a sense of guilt gnawing at me. It was my pillow, and Peter had taken the hit for it. He had done the time for something that was my fault. But he kept telling me not to worry about it. He said it wasn't my fault—he should have mailed it earlier. Still, I couldn't shake the feeling.

We spent the night at Cam Ranh Bay, and by some stroke of luck, there was a concert that night. We took Peter to the concert, and for the first time since I'd met him, I saw him smile. He seemed happy for just a little while, enjoying the music and the moment. It felt like a small mercy, a brief escape from what lay ahead. But the next morning, we had to put the handcuffs back on to make it look official.

We took him to Long Binh, and when we arrived at the gate, a Marine took the papers, called over two others, and they walked Peter away.

As we hugged to say goodbye, I saw tears in his eyes. I could feel the weight of the moment. I felt terrible. So, my fellow guard suggested we go to Saigon for the night—to try to cheer ourselves up.

We made it to the city, and the first thing we wanted was a drink. We found a bar and went in, but we didn't have much money. We could only afford one drink each. As soon as we sat down, two beautiful Vietnamese girls came over and sat at our table. They wanted us to buy them drinks, but we didn't have enough to cover even one round, let alone theirs. It wasn't very comfortable, especially since they didn't believe us when we said we didn't have the money.

Saigon Bar Girl

Now they wanted to come to our room. They were so stunning—so different from the girls we were used to up north. It felt like they were from another world entirely. We could barely afford the drinks, but they wanted to come with us. It was hard to turn them away, but we had no choice. It was one of those moments where you felt like everything was out of reach, everything was just a dream, just another thing slipping away.

The next day, we made our way back north. That was the last time I saw Peter. He was transferred to another unit after he got out of jail, and I never heard from him again.

Life moved on, but there was always that one moment—Peter, the pillow, the guilt. I couldn't help but wonder how things could have been different. Maybe if he had mailed it earlier, none of it would have happened. But it did, and I learned from it. The Nam has a way of making sure you never forget the mistakes you make, even if they're small ones.

Chapter 10
Bobby's Girl

We had been warned again and again not to get involved with a Vietnamese girl. There were a hundred reasons why it was a bad idea. The paperwork to bring her to The World—America—was massive. It wasn't just about the logistics; it was the never-ending red tape, the background checks, the interviews, the waiting. It could take years to sort out, and by the time it was all done, maybe things would have changed. And that wasn't even the biggest problem. The real issue was that if you married a Vietnamese woman, you were essentially giving her a ticket to America. She'd be able to escape her life here, to start over in the States, leaving everything behind. It was a dream for many of them, and a dangerous one for the soldiers. It wasn't the kind of thing that anyone wanted to get involved in, but sometimes, things didn't work out the way we planned.

Bobby was a good guy. Everybody liked him—he had that way about him, easygoing and always with a smile. He could make friends with anyone, and people were naturally drawn to him. He wasn't the type of guy to get bogged down by the war; he seemed to glide through everything with an easy grace. It wasn't that he was naive—he had seen enough to know what was going on—but he had a way of finding joy in the little things, and people appreciated that about him. It was like he had this gift to lighten the mood, even when things were at their darkest.

One evening, Bobby came to me and asked if I could take him through the wire that night. I understood what he was asking. Going through the wire wasn't a simple walk around camp—it was a risky journey. The wire was the barricade that separated us from the outside world. It stretched around the base, thick and tightly wound, and the only way to get past it was to crawl through it at the airfield. It led to a small village on the outskirts where local women lived. The girls there, desperate for a way out of their lives, often found themselves spending time with soldiers, offering comfort for a price. The trade was simple enough—money in exchange for the company, for a night away from the madness.

I'd been through the wire a few times, and the trek was always risky. The guards at the airfield were often on edge, drunk or smoking late into the night, and sometimes they could mistake us for the Viet Cong. It wasn't just the guards you had to worry about—it was everything. The noise of the night, the rustling in the brush, the strange sounds of the jungle that could play tricks on your mind. But Bobby trusted me. I was a frequent visitor to the village, and he knew I had the experience.

That night, we made our way to the airfield, crossing the runway quietly, our boots barely making a sound. When we got to the guard tower, we had to tell the guards that we'd be coming back through the wire in the morning and that they shouldn't shoot us. It was always a tricky thing to explain. You never knew how the guards would react, and even though they'd let us through, there was always that uneasy feeling that something could go wrong at any moment. I remember the guards, half asleep, nodding as we told them our plan. It was a dangerous trip, no matter how many times you did it. But Bobby wanted to go, and I wasn't about to leave him to go alone.

Once we made it through the wire, Bobby met a girl almost immediately. She was young and pretty, with dark eyes and a shy smile. It was clear that something clicked between them almost instantly. He seemed to fall for her right away, and she, in turn, appeared to take a liking to him. It wasn't hard to see why. Bobby had a charm that made people feel comfortable around him, and I could tell that the girl liked the attention. He went with her to the small house where she worked.

I told Bobby I'd see him in the morning. It was a routine by then—I'd spend the night with the other guys, and Bobby would have his time with her. For $20, you could spend the night with the girl and get a rather large joint as part of the deal. It wasn't much, but it made the nights a little more bearable. The things you did to survive, right? But there was something about that night that felt different. Bobby really took to the girl. He went back often, spending more and more time with her. I could see the way he looked at her, how she made him smile in a way that was rare around here. She wasn't just a girl to him—she was something more.

One night, a few of us went through the wire together, just for a change of pace. The evening was peaceful—no trouble, just good company and the simple pleasure of being away from the constant hum of the base. I was feeling excellent that night, in a way that made me forget about the war, the tension, the violence that we carried with us every day. It was one of those rare moments when things felt normal, when we could pretend for just a little while that everything was okay.

But then, everything changed. The door to the house burst open, and one of the guys came rushing in, his face white with panic. "Bobby's in trouble!" he said. I didn't wait to hear any more. I ran straight out of the house, not even thinking about what I was doing. I knew where Bobby would be, and I headed toward that place without hesitation.

I ran into the house and found myself in the middle of chaos. On one side was Bobby, his face streaked with tears, in a state of distress like I had never seen before. On the other side was the girl, crying as well, holding a knife in her hand. Around them, her family was shouting, all at once, in a blur of angry voices. The scene was pure confusion—a storm of emotions, fear, and rage. I had no idea what was going on at first, but I knew I had to get Bobby out of there.

I walked over to him, trying to calm him down, and I told him to come with me. We needed to leave before things got worse. I led him outside, away from the chaos, and sat with him in the quiet of the night. After a few moments, when his breathing slowed and he started to regain his composure, I asked him what had happened.

Bobby wiped his eyes and told me what had gone wrong. He had asked the girl to marry him. He was serious about it, or at least he thought he was. But she had refused, and that rejection sparked a huge argument between them. In the heat of the moment, she had pulled a knife on him. The whole thing had gotten out of control, escalating too quickly. The experience shook Bobby. He wasn't physically hurt, but the emotional blow had been enough to send him into a panic.

It took a while, but Bobby was okay in time. The shock wore off, and he started to recover from the incident. But something had changed in him after that night. He never went through the wire again. It was as if the innocence had been stripped away from him in a single, sharp moment. He had gone there seeking comfort, and instead, he found pain. It was strange how being here, in The Nam, affected your mind. You didn't think clearly all the time. Things became clouded. Maybe that's why Bobby had gone through the wire in the first place—to escape the chaos in his mind, to find something normal, something real. But instead, he found something else entirely.

After all, this was The Nam. And nothing ever worked out the way you expected.

Chapter 11
Hanoi Hannah

After some time in Vietnam, I began to tire of carrying the radio. The constant weight of it, the responsibility to keep it on me, became exhausting. I had enlisted with the intention of working on radios, of being a radio repairman, but somehow I ended up stuck carrying a radio out in the field instead. One day, I decided I couldn't take it anymore. I went to see the company commander to tell him my story. I explained why I enlisted, my training, and how I really wanted to work in a communications shack, fixing radios like I had trained for.

He listened patiently, and after a moment of contemplation, he told me that he would transfer me to a communications shack where I could work on radios. I was relieved, though I knew the job wouldn't be glamorous. The shack wasn't exactly bustling with work. There were only two other radio repairmen attached to the shack, and with so few radios needing fixing, we ended up doing odd jobs. Sometimes, we filled sandbags or cleaned the shack, which wasn't exactly what I had hoped for, but at least it was out of the field. We also had to take turns working the switchboard, sitting there and transferring calls as they came in. It was tedious work, but at least I wasn't out on patrol anymore.

One night, I was on duty at the switchboard. It was unusually quiet, the kind of quiet that made the night feel even heavier. I was listening to the Armed Forces Network on the radio, passing the time. Then, suddenly, a woman's voice broke through. It wasn't the usual broadcast. The voice was calm but chilling as she spoke. She warned Americans that they should leave or they were all going to die. She mentioned the names of Americans who had been captured and others who had been killed.

The woman identified herself as Hanoi Hannah. I was stunned. I had heard of her before, but hearing her voice in that moment, so clear and direct, was a shock. Her real name was Trinh Thi Ngo, and she worked for the People's Army of Vietnam. She was essentially a propaganda tool, reading scripts handed to her by the North Vietnamese. But she was very effective. Her words got under your skin like a slow burn.

She was just like Tokyo Rose during World War II—another voice who sought to disrupt morale and weaken the resolve of American soldiers. She would often try to persuade Americans to leave their posts, telling them they didn't belong there. Hanoi Hannah even played tapes of captured Americans who had been tortured into admitting that America had no business being in Vietnam. Those voices were enough to make anyone question their place there, and she knew how to use them.

Hanoi Hannah

It wasn't long before we were officially told to ignore her broadcasts. We were told that it was just North Vietnamese propaganda, a strategy to manipulate our minds. But it wasn't that easy. Morale began to decline across the base, especially after hearing her voice. Every time we tuned in, her words echoed in our minds.

I decided it was time for a break, a real one. I had heard of R&R (rest and recuperation), a brief leave soldiers were allowed during their time in Vietnam. You couldn't go back to the States for your R&R, but you could go to places like Japan, Bangkok, Australia, or Hawaii. My buddy and I, both from LA, decided we would go to Hawaii. The idea of getting away from the war, if only for a short while, was a lifeline.

We made it through the application process, and it turned out we were lucky enough to be on the last flight to Hawaii for single men. They had started allowing only married men to go to Hawaii to meet their wives, but somehow, we cut.

We arrived in Hawaii and quickly changed into civilian clothes, our nerves high with excitement and anxiety. We purchased our tickets to LA, and it worked. We were going home—at least for a little while.

The seven-day leave was short, but it was all we had. My parents were thrilled to see me. My mom made a nice dinner, and they invited a few of my friends over. It was good to be home, but I couldn't shake the feeling that something was wrong. Sleeping in my bed felt strange. It was too soft, too comfortable. Sitting at the dinner table felt like an alien experience.

The whole time, I couldn't stop thinking about The Nam, about what I had left behind. I kept my feelings to myself, as hard as it was. The visitors eventually left, and the house became quiet. My parents asked me about my time in Vietnam, but I couldn't talk about it. I didn't know how to explain it, not in a way they would understand. So they asked me, "What do you want to do?"

I told them I wanted to go to Canada. My mother didn't hesitate. She immediately started making phone calls, reaching out to relatives in Montreal. They offered me a job and a place to stay. Everything was set, except one thing: I had to tell my buddy that I wasn't going back with him.

I called him up to let him know. We talked for over two hours. In the end, he convinced me that Canada wasn't the answer. "If you leave like this, you'll never be allowed to come back," he said. He made me see that leaving would mean cutting myself off from everything I knew. He convinced me to return with him to Vietnam.

My parents were upset, of course. They were worried about me, about how I was acting—withdrawn, sleeping on the floor instead of in my bed. They urged me to see someone, to talk about it, but I couldn't. I didn't want to talk to anyone. The Nam had changed me. I wasn't sure how to handle it or how to move forward. I needed time to figure it out.

We were supposed to return to Vietnam in just seven days, but now we were one day late. My buddy and I decided to stay in Hawaii for a couple of extra days, as cheap as things were for servicemen. We stayed at the Hilton on the beach for almost nothing. The days passed, and I told him I wasn't ready to leave just yet. We stayed one more night. Then the next day, I told him again I wasn't ready to leave. By now, we were four days late.

We decided to leave the next morning, but the plane we were supposed to be on had already left. We couldn't just book another flight—who would fly to a war zone? So, we made our way to an Air Force base nearby and spoke to the flight marshal. We told him our situation—how we were five days late—and he said there was a flight tomorrow, and he'd try to get us on it.

But the next day, the flight was full. So, we waited another day. Same result. There was no room for us. We were out of money and out of options. The marshal told us that there was a plane leaving right then, but it was a cargo plane heading to the Philippines. We decided to take it. We ran out to the runway, the back of the plane opened, and we jumped on. No seats, just boxes. We sat on the floor seven days late.

The next stop was the Philippines. We got there, but all the planes coming in were full of troops heading to Vietnam. After another couple of days, we finally got on a flight and landed in the south of Vietnam. From there, it took another two days to get to our unit. When we finally walked into the command center to sign in, we were nine days late.

The first sergeant looked at us, his face cold and stern. "You went home, didn't you?" There was a long pause.

"Yes, we did," I answered.

Another long pause, and then he finally said, "Get the fuck out of my office."

Chapter 12
Australia

With about 100 days left in my tour, I decided to take some time off and go on leave to Australia. I don't remember much of that trip—it's all kind of a blur, honestly. What I do remember most is how tired I was, both mentally and physically. I was exhausted. My mind and body had been running on empty for so long that all I could do was sleep. And that's exactly what I did. I slept and slept, trying to process everything I had been through, everything I had seen, and things I hadn't even mentioned in this book.

I did manage to take a quick tour of Sydney. The sights were beautiful, but I was in no state to really take them in. The city felt like a foreign world to me. I went to a club one night, hoping to enjoy the night out, but the loud music and crowds were too much. I wasn't used to being around so many people anymore. The noise, the laughter, the conversations—it all felt overwhelming, almost suffocating. The loudness was like a constant pressure on my chest, reminding me of the chaos I had left behind, and somehow, I felt more at home in the quiet tension of The Nam.

In a way, I was relieved when the week was over, and I could head back. Back to what I knew. The familiarity of the base, the routine, the dangers. It felt strange to think that I felt more comfortable there than I did in a place like Sydney. I wasn't the only one who felt this way. I heard it from other soldiers too. We had all been through too much, and there was a strange sense of disconnection between us and the outside world. The World, as we called it, seemed so far away, so different. Perhaps it was because we weren't welcome back. Back home, they called us "baby killers," a label that haunted us. It was tied to the villages that were burned and to the atrocities like the My Lai massacre, where Americans wiped out an entire village. That was the stigma we came home to, and it made it hard to fit back in.

The trip to Australia didn't change me. If anything, it made me more aware of how much I had changed. I didn't like the person I had become, but I couldn't change it overnight. Maybe in time, I would find a way to heal. Or perhaps it wouldn't last. Who could say?

I was headed back to Vietnam. Only thirty days left in The Nam. They called it "short time"—a term that meant you were nearing the end of your tour. You could see the finish line, but it was still far enough away to feel like a struggle.

We landed at Cam Ranh Bay, and I decided to stay there for a few days before heading back to my unit. I bumped into a guy from my company, someone I recognized but didn't know well. He asked me what I was doing, and I told him I was staying in Cam Ranh Bay for a couple of days. He looked at me with a strange expression and said, "You better get back."

"Why? What's going on?" I asked, confused.

He just smiled and said, "You better get back." He wouldn't tell me why. Something in his tone made me uneasy, but I took his advice. I packed up and headed north to my camp.

When I arrived at the command post, I signed in and handed my papers to the clerk. He gave me a sign-in form, and then, with a strange look on his face, he said, "Now, sign this. Your sign-out papers."

"What? Where am I going?" I asked, a little shocked.

"You're going home, radio man," he said, handing me the papers.

I couldn't believe it. I was being sent home 30 days early. I wasn't about to argue with that. I said my goodbyes, packed my stuff and caught a flight back to Cam Ranh Bay to process out. It took about four days, but finally, I was cleared to leave.

We were all anxious, desperate to get on that plane, to leave The Nam behind. This adventure—this nightmare—was over. But even as I left, I couldn't help but feel the weight of everything that had happened. The scar that The Nam had left on me was still there, and I knew it would stay with me long after I was back home.

On the plane, I looked out the window and thought about everything I wanted to remember about The Nam and, more importantly, the things I wanted to forget. There were moments that I would carry with me for the rest of my life, but there were also things I wished I could erase from my memory.

The pic really shows the jubilation of going home.

When the plane left the ground, there was a loud cheer from the men aboard. The jubilation was raw, honest, and contagious. The cheers echoed through the cabin, the relief palpable in the air. It wasn't just about leaving the war behind—it was about the freedom of going home. It was a feeling I could never put into words, but the picture in my mind was clear: we were going home.

Chapter 13
Returning Home

The airplane finally landed at Fort Lewis, Washington, and as I stepped off the plane, a feeling of mixed emotions overwhelmed me. It was a strange and unfamiliar sensation. I had just completed my tour of duty in Vietnam and was now back in the United States. I had survived, but my journey wasn't over yet. The military greeted us with a warm welcome and even treated us to a steak dinner. It felt strange—so normal, so different from what I had just been through. The men around me were all in various stages of exhaustion, their faces showing signs of the long months we had endured.

After the meal, the military officials divided us into two groups. One group was free. They were done with their service. They had completed their duty, and now they were free to go home, to be with their families, to start a new chapter of their lives. The other group, which included me, still had more time to serve. We were sent to another post to continue our duty.

As I looked at the men who were being released, I felt a mix of envy and sadness. They were free, and I wasn't. The thought of having to stay in the military for another 18 months made me feel like my soul was heavy. My body was tired, and my mind was weary. I had just returned from the horrors of war, and all I wanted was to be home, to feel the safety of familiar surroundings. But here I was, still bound to the military, still locked in a life I didn't want. It was hard to accept that I had to keep going while they got to leave, to walk away from the past.

Eventually, they handed us our new orders. The next stop for me was Fort Meade, Maryland. Maryland? I had to go all the way to the other side of the country. I had no choice. I couldn't understand why they couldn't post me somewhere closer, maybe somewhere I could reconnect with family, somewhere that felt like home. But no, I had to go to Maryland. I felt lost, like I had no control over my life.

I boarded a flight to Los Angeles, where I was given 30 days of leave. Thirty days to return home, to see my family, to find some semblance of peace. When I arrived at the airport, I took a cab to my house. But when I arrived, the house was empty. No one was there. My parents were still at work, so I decided to walk to my friend's house. I had been thinking about him a lot during my time away, and the thought of seeing him again filled me with hope.

When I knocked on the door, his mother answered, and when she saw me standing there, her eyes filled with tears. She couldn't believe it. She pulled me into a big hug, and before I could say a word, my friend came running out. He was the first person to hug me and say, "Welcome home." His voice cracked, and his hug felt like a lifeline, as if he understood everything I had been through. It was a bittersweet feeling. I was home, but I wasn't the same person who had left.

I asked my friend if he could drive me to my mother's workplace. She worked at a pharmacy, and I needed to pick up the key to the apartment. When we arrived, I walked in, but she wasn't at the front. The other clerk asked her to come up, and when she saw me, her face lit up. She screamed, "Is this a dream?" Then she rushed toward me and pulled me into a tight embrace. There, in her arms, I felt a wave of emotion wash over me. I had made it back, but it wasn't as simple as I had hoped. I could see in her eyes that she had no idea when I would return, and my sudden appearance was a complete surprise.

The following 30 days went by in a blur. It felt like time was moving too quickly, and yet, at the same time, it felt like I couldn't escape the weight of the past. My parents noticed that I was different. I wasn't the same person who had left. I was quieter now, more withdrawn. I couldn't find the right words to explain what I had been through, what I was feeling. It was like I was living in a world that no longer made sense. My emotions were a whirlwind—there was a constant struggle inside me like I was caught between two different lives, neither of which felt real.

During this time, I learned something that shocked me. President Nixon had ordered that all troops who had 30 days or less left in their service were to be sent home early. It made me question everything. Why had I not known this before? Was my early return just a coincidence? I wasn't sure how to process it. I had come home early, but for what reason? Was it because of the war, because of what we had all been through? Or was it just a political decision that didn't mean anything?

As the days passed, I started to feel more and more like I was living in the past. The weight of Vietnam was still with me, clinging to my every thought. I needed to do something, to escape for a little while, to clear my head. So, I decided to buy a car. I would drive to Maryland, across the country. It was a long trip, but I hoped it would give me the time I needed to think to figure things out.

The drive was exhausting, but it gave me something I hadn't had in a long time—time to think, time to reflect. Along the way, I met people, strangers who were kind and welcoming. I stopped at diners, at gas stations and spoke with people who shared stories of their own lives. I needed those moments of connection. They helped me feel human again, like I wasn't just a soldier but a person with a past, a person who was more than what the war had made of me.

Every mile I drove, I thought about Vietnam, about The Nam. It was hard to escape it, hard to forget. Sometimes, it felt like it never happened, like it was just a dream or a nightmare. But deep down, I knew it wasn't. It had happened, and now I had to find a way to move forward, to live a life beyond the war. The trip wasn't just about the miles—it was about finding myself again. It was about understanding that I was more than the things I had seen and done. It was about healing.

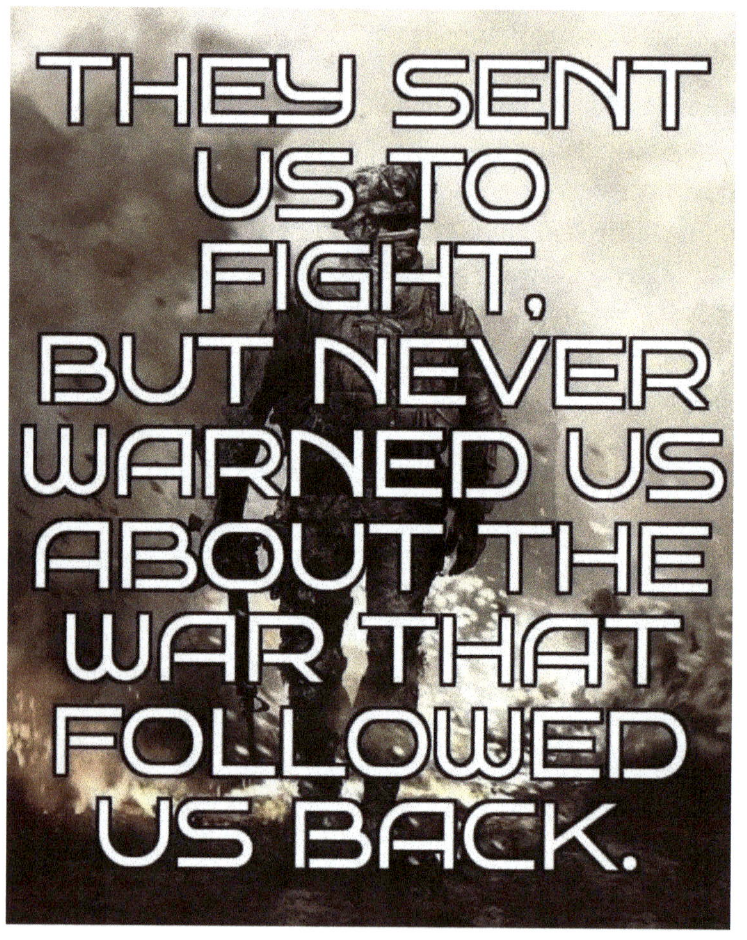

Chapter 14
Fort Meade

When I finally arrived at Fort Meade, I felt a mixture of exhaustion and confusion. I had just completed a long and tiring journey, and now I had to adjust to my new life here. I parked my car and got out, standing still for a moment. I couldn't help but just stare at the barracks in front of me. It felt strange to be back in the United States, but I couldn't shake the heavy feeling in my chest. The barracks reminded me of basic training, the long hours, the discipline, and the nervous anticipation. All of it came rushing back, and I couldn't push away the bad feeling that hung over me.

I didn't want to be here. Fort Meade seemed like another place where I had to keep pretending, pretending that everything was fine, when deep down, I was anything but fine. I felt stuck. I had no choice but to continue with my orders, but I couldn't help the dread that lingered.

I found where my barracks were and went inside to sign in. I gave them my papers, and they took care of the formalities. Then I decided to go into town for lunch. I was hungry, but more than that, I needed a break from the constant tension, from the pressure that came with being surrounded by people who had no idea what I had been through. While I was in town, I remembered something that someone had told me: that if you didn't like where you were, you could go to the Pentagon and try to get your orders changed. Maybe this was my chance to escape, to find a way out of this place.

Car I Drove Across the County

So, that afternoon, I decided to drive to the Pentagon. As soon as I got there, I realized just how big and overwhelming it was. The building was huge, and the hallways seemed to stretch endlessly in every direction. It felt like a maze. I was walking through the halls, desperately looking for the office I needed, but everything seemed confusing. The noise, the crowds, the sense of urgency everywhere— it was all too much.

After what felt like hours, I stumbled upon a stairway and decided to take a break. I needed a moment to breathe, to gather my thoughts. I sat down, feeling the weight of everything pressing down on me. The silence of the stairwell was a relief. For a brief moment, I was able to think clearly, away from the chaos.

Then, the door to the stairwell opened, and a sergeant walked in. He noticed me sitting there and asked if I needed help. I felt a bit embarrassed, but I told him what I was looking for. He nodded and said, "Oh, that office is right down the hall." He led me to the office, and I thanked him for his help.

I walked into the office with a small glimmer of hope, thinking that maybe I could finally get something changed. I told the clerk that I wanted a transfer to a base closer to home. He didn't even look up at first, but then he said, "No problem. Just give me your file."

My stomach sank. I realized that I had already signed in at Fort Meade, and without that file, there was nothing anyone could do. The clerk looked at me, and his eyes said it all. "There's nothing I can do without your file," he said.

I felt my heart drop. I had come all this way for nothing. Disappointment washed over me as I turned and walked out of the Pentagon, the weight of failure heavy on my shoulders. I got back into my car and drove back to Fort Meade. It was a long drive back, and I felt like I had lost more than just time. I had lost my hope for change.

When I got back to the barracks, I was placed in a room with other guys who had never been to The Nam. They were curious, asking me question after question, wanting to know what it had been like. I didn't want to talk about it. I didn't want to relive those memories. But they kept pushing, and I just didn't have the strength to explain. It was easier to stay quiet.

I couldn't sleep in that bed with the sheets they gave me, so I stripped the bed down and used a poncho I had kept from The Nam. It was something familiar, something that still connected me to the past, and it made me feel just a little bit safer. But the other guys didn't understand. They thought I was strange, and it only made me feel more isolated. They eventually gave me a room to myself. I didn't mind. It meant I didn't have to deal with their questions or their pity. I was alone, and that was what I needed.

Every morning, a jeep would come to pick me up and take me to the ranges. There, I would get on a tractor and spend the day cutting grass. It was a simple task, but I didn't mind. The repetitive motion of driving the tractor gave me a chance to think, to escape my mind. I'd smoke marijuana, trying to numb the pain, to forget everything for a little while. It helped, but it didn't fix anything. Nothing could.

I didn't want to talk to anyone. I just wanted to be left alone, and I found that the tractor was my escape. It was my salvation, a way to avoid the world and everything in it. No one bothered me when I was on that tractor. I could just zone out, my mind wandering while I cut the grass. But even in those moments, there was a problem. I felt like no one cared about me. No one offered to help, and I didn't know how to ask for help. It felt like I was utterly alone in a world that didn't understand me.

After work, I'd get taken back to the barracks, but I didn't stay long. I'd change my clothes, and then I would just leave. I didn't want to be there. I didn't want to be around anyone. I needed to drive, to clear my mind, to think about what was next. I had no idea what I was going to do after I was discharged. I didn't know how to fix myself, how to feel normal again.

The guys in the barracks noticed me, of course. They were curious. "Who is that guy who gets picked up every morning and dropped off at night?" they asked. They would approach me, trying to figure me out, but I never told them anything. I wasn't ready to talk. Over time, I became friendly with a couple of them, but we never talked about The Nam. They didn't ask, and I didn't offer. We kept it that way.

Eight months had passed, and I still had one more year of military service left. The time dragged on, but during that time, I started thinking about my future. I didn't want to stay in the military forever. I wanted something else. I decided that I wanted to go back to school.

I thought about becoming a teacher. I had always been good at sports, so I figured I could become a physical education teacher. It was a way to imagine a different life, a life where I wasn't stuck in the past. It felt like a small dream, something I could hold onto. But for now, the only thing I had to look forward to was driving the tractor every day.

71

Chapter 15
Carol

The weekends were always the hardest for me. Most of the guys would go home, and the barracks would become eerily quiet. It felt empty, almost like the building was mourning, and it only added to the loneliness I was already feeling.

What I usually did to get away from that silence was drive to the University of Maryland. There was always something going on there—parties, events, people gathering. I didn't care much about the details. I'd show up, act like I belonged, and offer someone a joint. If they took it, I knew I was in. I just wanted to be around people, to feel like I was a part of something, even if it was just for a few hours.

One weekend, something different happened. I noticed a girl sitting by herself. She was incredibly pretty—so much so that I couldn't help but be drawn to her. For some reason, I felt like I should talk to her. I gathered my courage and walked over. I started a conversation, and she was so receptive, so easy to talk to. It felt like we had known each other forever. We hit it off right away, and we started seeing each other every weekend after that.

Her name was Carol. She was kind, intelligent, and her smile made everything feel right, even when the world felt upside down. We didn't always have the money for a hotel, but Carol would sneak me into her dorm room, and we'd just hang out together. It was simple, but in those moments, I didn't need anything else.

One weekend, Carol told me that she had to leave the dorm because her parents were going away. They lived not too far from the university, and they were going to Virginia Beach for a week. She asked me to stay at the house with her while they were gone. I was thrilled and said yes right away.

When I got to her place, I couldn't believe it. The house was huge, beautiful, and located in a very upscale neighborhood. Everything about it felt different from the barracks and the world I had been living in. It was nice to be there, like stepping into another world, one that felt like it was full of possibility.

But nothing could stay perfect for long. On Saturday night, I said I should go back to the base because Carol's parents were due to return the next day. She told me not to worry—they wouldn't be back until late. I felt relieved and decided to stay. But the next morning, I woke up to the sound of footsteps running up the stairs. My heart sank. Carol burst into the room, panic in her eyes. "They're back!" she said.

Not only were her parents home, but her mother was headed upstairs to check on things. Carol told me to hide, and quickly, I started to get dressed. But I didn't have time. I had to think fast—under the bed or in the closet? I chose the closet.

I ran inside, completely naked, and knelt down, hoping she wouldn't find me. I held my breath as the door to the room opened just a crack. I could hear her moving around the room. She checked under the bed, then left. I thought I had made it, but just as I was about to get my clothes, the mother came in again. She went straight for the closet.

She tried to open the door, but I was holding it shut with everything I had. I was terrified, and then I realized it was no use. She knew I was in there. With a deep breath, I let the door go, and it opened.

There I was, kneeling on the floor, trying to cover myself as best I could. She looked down at me, and her eyes filled with tears. The moment felt like it lasted forever. She ran out of the room, and I heard her yell downstairs, "Jerry, there's a naked man upstairs!" My heart raced. What would happen now?

I didn't know what to expect. Was her father going to come up here and punch me in the nose? That's what I would've expected, and honestly, I probably would've felt better if he did. But instead, I heard him coming up the stairs. He walked into the room. He was short, wearing glasses. Not what I had imagined at all.

He didn't hit me. Instead, he looked at me, and after a long pause, he said, "Are you ready to leave?" I looked at him, stunned, and replied, "Yes, sir." It was strange, but I think he appreciated the respect I showed him. It was as if, in that moment, he realized I was taking responsibility for what had happened.

We left the room together, and when we got to the top of the stairs, Carol's mother was standing at the bottom, looking up at me. She pointed at me and said, "What right do you have to come into my house, you son of a bitch?" I didn't say a word. There was nothing I could say.

Then she held up a check. It was meant for Carol's next semester at school, but she ripped it up right in front of us. "You can forget about this," she said. There was nothing left to say. We walked out of the house, leaving everything behind.

I felt terrible. Carol had lost her tuition, and now her family was falling apart. I felt like I was responsible for everything. The only way to fix it, I thought, was to marry Carol. If I married her, it would make everything right. She would be with her family again, and they'd help pay for her schooling.

Carol told her parents, and they wanted to meet me. I didn't know how to feel about it, but I decided to go through with it. I needed to face them and try to make things right. The meeting was tense. We sat in the living room as they asked me all kinds of questions about my family, my plans, and my future. It felt like I was on trial, but I answered as best as I could.

Over time, things started to get better. Carol and I were spending more time together, and I began to feel like we were getting closer. But I wasn't sure if I wanted to get married yet. It wasn't about her; it was about me. I wasn't ready for that kind of commitment.

One Saturday afternoon, I was sitting with Carol's father watching a hockey game. Carol and her mother had gone out shopping, and Carol said, "We're just going to look at wedding dresses." I laughed, thinking it was no big deal. "Don't buy anything," I told her. She just smiled and said, "No, we're just looking." I said it again, "Don't buy anything."

A little while later, they returned. Carol looked at me with a huge grin and said, "I have a surprise! I bought a wedding dress!" My face dropped. Now I was really stuck. There was no way out.

That night, I drove Carol back to the dorm, kissed her goodbye, and drove off, feeling like I was trapped. At the same time, my parents were moving back to Montreal and wanted to stop by and see me in Fort Meade. I told them good because I have something to say to them. I didn't want to tell them yet, but I knew I had to. When they arrived, my father knew what was coming. He asked me one question: "Do you love her?" I looked at him, but I couldn't answer. He nodded, and we didn't talk about it again.

Two days later, my parents left for Montreal, and I was left to make a decision. I liked Carol, but I wasn't ready for marriage. She had made my time in the service bearable, and we had fun together, but I wasn't sure I wanted to settle down just yet.

I told her there would be no wedding. She didn't take it well. It was hard for both of us, but I had to leave. I was done with the service, and I wanted to be free to do what I wanted. I had enough adventure for now. I decided to apply to college in Montreal. My parents were there, and I could always go back to L.A. later if I wanted.

Two weeks before I was discharged, I was getting ready to leave when a car pulled in and blocked my way. It was Carol. She came up to my car and said, "I have something to tell you." She paused, and then she said, "I'm pregnant."

I was stunned. "Oh Carol, don't do this to me," I said. "I'm leaving in two weeks. I'm going to Montreal." We talked for a while longer, but I knew I had to go. I received my discharge and moved to Montreal to finish my degree.

I eventually found a teaching job on a native reserve and married a native girl. We had two boys, and they gave us eleven grandchildren and three great-grandchildren. Sometimes, I think about the past, about Carol, about the choices I made. It seems like a lifetime ago, but at the same time, it feels like yesterday.

I never had flashbacks, but the memories still linger. And in some ways, I feel lucky. I was one of the lucky ones who made it out of The Nam. But one thing still hurts, even now: the way we were treated when we came home. There was no warm welcome, no recognition. We did what the government asked us to do, and all we got was a form letter from President Nixon thanking us for our service. The irony is that I ended up in Canada. I never wanted to go to Canada, and yet here I am.

In time, I received a letter from Carol telling me she wasn't pregnant after all.

What We Never Received

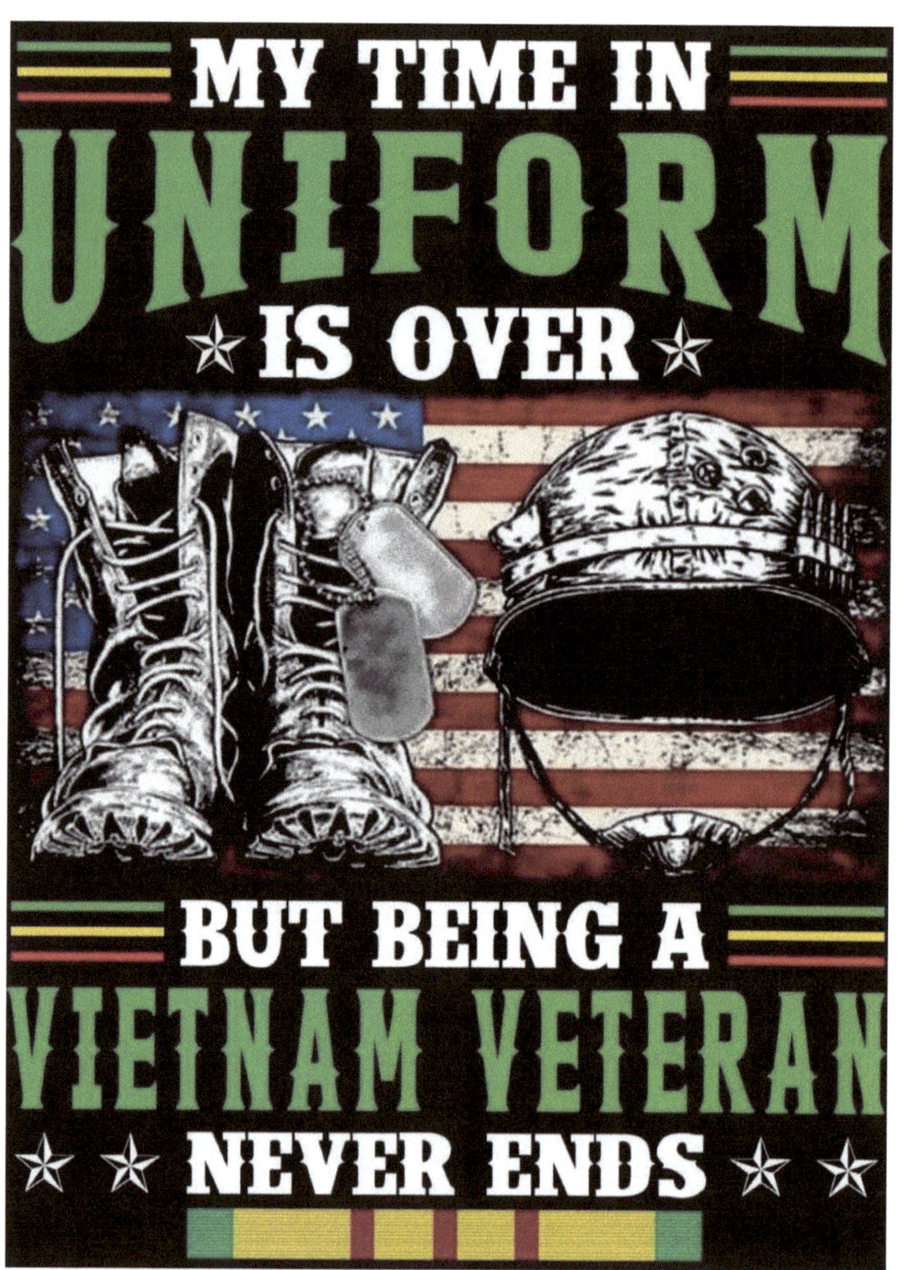

MY TIME IN
UNIFORM
★ IS OVER ★
BUT BEING A
VIETNAM VETERAN
NEVER ENDS